MR. BROWN'S BAD DAY

To my lovely dad, who is my best
kind of very important person xx – LP
For Kitt x – AF

Text by Lou Peacock
Text copyright © 2020
by Nosy Crow Ltd.
Illustrations copyright
© 2020 by Alison Friend
Nosy Crow and its logos are
trademarks of Nosy Crow Ltd.
Used under license.

First US edition 2020

Library of Congress Catalog
Card Number pending
ISBN 978-1-5362-1436-9

20 21 22 23 24 25 WKT 10 9 8 7 6 5 4 3 2 1

Printed in Shenzhen,
Guangdong, China

This book was
typeset in Bodoni.
The illustrations
were done in
mixed media.

Nosy Crow
an imprint of
Candlewick Press
99 Dover Street
Somerville,
Massachusetts 02144

www.nosycrow.com
www.candlewick.com

MR. BROWN'S BAD DAY

LOU PEACOCK

illustrated by
ALISON FRIEND

nosy crow™

An imprint of Candlewick Press

Mr. Brown was a very important businessman.
He always carried a very important briefcase,
and he worked in a very important office.

He said things like "Sell! Sell!"
   Though sometimes he said, "Buy! Buy!"

People brought him important papers to sign,
and he went to lots and lots of meetings.

Mr. Brown was always very, very busy.

But no matter how busy he was, Mr. Brown always went out for lunch.

Naturally, Mr. Brown took his very important briefcase.

It had very important things in it, after all.

Mr. Brown set the briefcase down, and as he ate his lunch,
he thought about very important things.

But because Mr. Brown was so busy thinking, he didn't notice a baby grabbing the handle of his very important briefcase. And he didn't notice the baby taking the very important briefcase away.

Suddenly, Mr. Brown realized that the very important briefcase was missing!

"My briefcase!" he said. "I must find it. It's full of very important things."

Fortunately for Mr. Brown, the baby
and the briefcase were not far away . . .

but unfortunately
for Mr. Brown,

the briefcase got hooked onto an ice cream cart . . .

and the ice cream seller pedaled away!

"Wait!" called Mr. Brown. "Wait!
That's my very important briefcase!"
Fortunately for Mr. Brown, the ice cream
seller soon stopped . . .

but unfortunately for Mr. Brown,
some schoolchildren accidentally
took the briefcase for a ride.

"Wait!" shouted Mr. Brown. "Wait!
That's my very important briefcase!"

Fortunately for Mr. Brown, the line was moving quickly . . .

but unfortunately for Mr. Brown,
when the schoolchildren got off the ride,
they took Mr. Brown's very important
briefcase with them.

And then they went to catch the bus.

"WAIT!" bellowed Mr. Brown. "WAIT!
That's my very important briefcase!"

Mr. Brown ran as fast as he could to the bus stop . . .

and was just in time to see the bus pull away.

Poor Mr. Brown.

His hat and jacket were gone and his tie was askew.
"This," said Mr. Brown, "is a very bad day."
But the very important briefcase was full of
very important things, so . . .

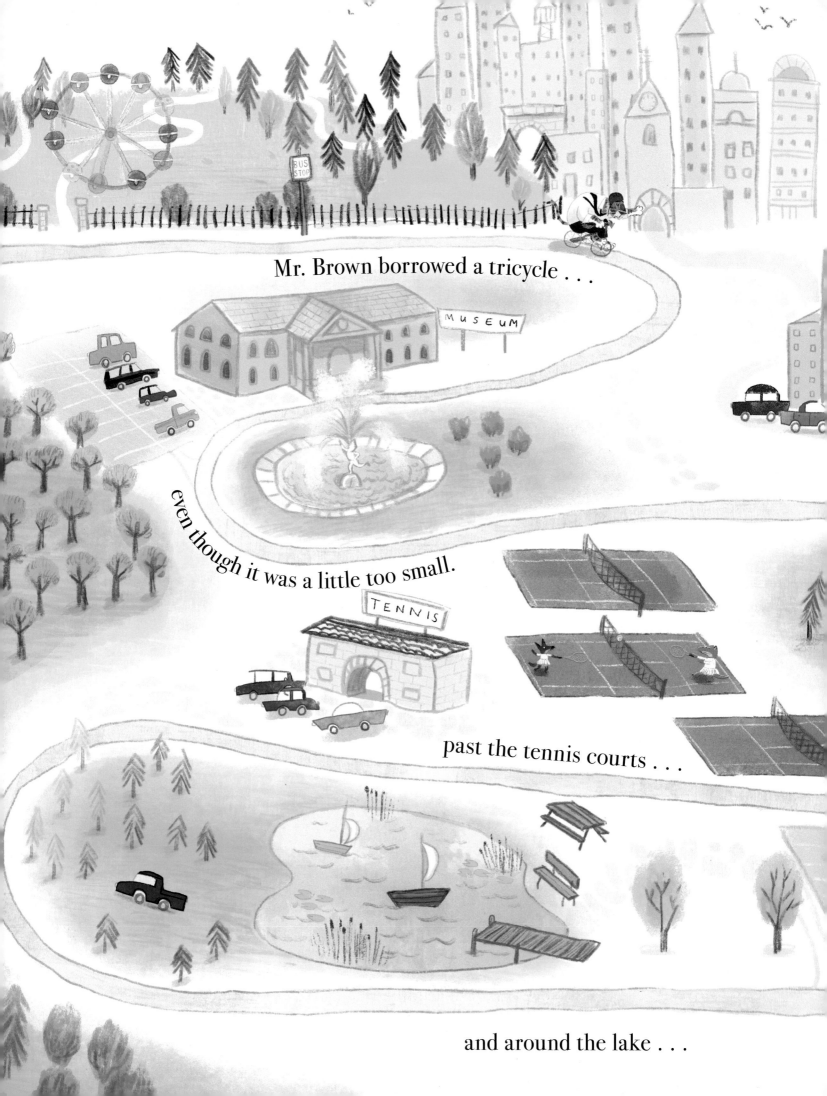

Mr. Brown borrowed a tricycle . . .

MUSEUM

even though it was a little too small.

TENNIS

past the tennis courts . . .

and around the lake . . .

He followed the bus all over town . . .

but he could never quite catch up.

When the children got off the bus, they took
the very important briefcase with them.

"Whose bag is this?" asked the teacher.

"Not mine,"
said one child.

"Not mine,"
said another.

"Or mine,"
said a third.

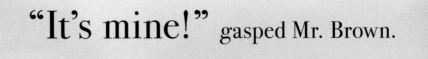

"It's mine!" gasped Mr. Brown.

"And there are very important things inside!"

By now, it was dark, and because it was too late to go back to his very important office, Mr. Brown went home.

When he got there, Mr. Brown opened his very important briefcase and checked that all the very important things were still inside it . . .

his snuggly blanket,

his book of
bedtime stories,

and his favorite teddy bear.

Then, with all the very
important things safe and
sound,

Mr. Brown settled down to the very
important business of . . .

bedtime.